Robin and the Monk

Tales of Robin Hood

First published in 2006 by
Franklin Watts
338 Euston Road
London
NW1 3BH

Franklin Watts Australia
Hachette Children's Books
Level 17/207 Kent Street
Sydney
NSW 2000

A CIP catalogue record for this book is available from the British Library.

ISBN (10) 0 7496 6687 0 (hbk)
ISBN (13) 978-0-7496-6687-3 (hbk)
ISBN (10) 0 7496 6700 1 (pbk)
ISBN (13) 978-0-7496-6700-9 (pbk)

Series Editor: Jackie Hamley
Series Advisor: Dr Barrie Wade
Series Designer: Peter Scoulding

Printed in China

Franklin Watts is a division of Hachette Children's Books.

Robin and the Monk

by Damian Harvey and Martin Remphry

Robin Hood and Little John were going to Nottingham. Robin wanted to visit St Mary's church.

As they walked, they played shooting for pennies.
The person that shot nearest the penny was the winner.

Little John had won five pennies
and Robin had won none.

After one game, the friends started arguing. "You cheated," said Robin. "I never cheat," cried Little John.

"And, for saying that, you can go to Nottingham by yourself!"

So Robin carried on alone.

At St Mary's church, lots of people recognised Robin.

As Robin knelt down to pray, one of the monks crept out of the church.

The monk ran as fast as he could to Nottingham castle.

"My lord Sheriff," cried the monk.

"Robin Hood is in the church.

You can catch him there."

When Robin left the church,
the Sheriff and his soldiers
were waiting for him.

“If only Little John were here to help!” thought Robin. “I wish we hadn’t argued!”

Robin fought bravely and swung his sword at the Sheriff. His sword hit the Sheriff's helmet and broke in two.

"Get him!" cried the Sheriff.
Robin tried to escape but the
Sheriff's men caught him.

The Sheriff of Nottingham
threw Robin into prison.

Then he sent the monk to tell
Prince John the good news.

As the monk travelled along the road, he met Little John. "Where are you going?" asked Little John.

"I'm off to tell Prince John that Robin Hood has been captured," said the monk.

Little John grabbed the monk.

"Robin Hood is my friend," he cried.

Little John took the monk's robes and tied him to a tree. "You can stay here," said Little John. "I'll go to see the Prince."

Prince John was so happy when Little John told him Robin was in prison that he gave him a bag of gold.

“Take this letter to the Sheriff,” said Prince John. “Then bring Robin Hood here.”

The Sheriff of Nottingham read Prince John's letter. "We will be rewarded for capturing Robin Hood," said the Sheriff.

"Let's have a feast to celebrate."

The Sheriff brought Robin out to see. "Look how we are celebrating your capture!" he teased. Then he threw Robin back into prison.

After the feast, the Sheriff and his men fell asleep.

While they slept, Little John rescued Robin.

They jumped down from the castle walls and ran to Sherwood Forest.

“We tricked Prince John and the Sheriff of Nottingham, and we got a bag of gold,” said Robin.

"Yes!" laughed Little John.
"And now we'll send this monk
back to Nottingham!"

Hopscotch has been specially designed to fit the requirements of the National Literacy Strategy. It offers real books by top authors and illustrators for children developing their reading skills.
There are 37 Hopscotch stories to choose from:

Marvin, the Blue Pig
ISBN 0 7496 4619 5

Plip and Plop
ISBN 0 7496 4620 9

The Queen's Dragon
ISBN 0 7496 4618 7

Flora McQuack
ISBN 0 7496 4621 7

Willie the Whale
ISBN 0 7496 4623 3

Naughty Nancy
ISBN 0 7496 4622 5

Run!
ISBN 0 7496 4705 1

The Playground Snake
ISBN 0 7496 4706 X

"Sausages!"
ISBN 0 7496 4707 8

The Truth about Hansel and Gretel
ISBN 0 7496 4708 6

Pippin's Big Jump
ISBN 0 7496 4710 8

Whose Birthday Is It?
ISBN 0 7496 4709 4

The Princess and the Frog
ISBN 0 7496 5129 6

Flynn Flies High
ISBN 0 7496 5130 X

Clever Cat
ISBN 0 7496 5131 8

Moo!
ISBN 0 7496 5332 9

Izzie's Idea
ISBN 0 7496 5334 5

Roly-poly Rice Ball
ISBN 0 7496 5333 7

I Can't Stand It!
ISBN 0 7496 5765 0

Cockerel's Big Egg
ISBN 0 7496 5767 7

How to Teach a Dragon Manners
ISBN 0 7496 5873 8

The Truth about those Billy Goats
ISBN 0 7496 5766 9

Marlowe's Mum and the Tree House
ISBN 0 7496 5874 6

Bear in Town
ISBN 0 7496 5875 4

The Best Den Ever
ISBN 0 7496 5876 2

ADVENTURE STORIES

Aladdin and the Lamp
ISBN 0 7496 6678 1 *
ISBN 0 7496 6692 7

Blackbeard the Pirate
ISBN 0 7496 6676 5 *
ISBN 0 7496 6690 0

George and the Dragon
ISBN 0 7496 6677 3 *
ISBN 0 7496 6691 9

Jack the Giant-Killer
ISBN 0 7496 6680 3 *
ISBN 0 7496 6693 5

TALES OF KING ARTHUR

1. The Sword in the Stone
ISBN 0 7496 6681 1 *
ISBN 0 7496 6694 3

2. Arthur the King
ISBN 0 7496 6683 8 *
ISBN 0 7496 6695 1

3. The Round Table
ISBN 0 7496 6684 6 *
ISBN 0 7496 6697 8

4. Sir Lancelot and the Ice Castle
ISBN 0 7496 6685 4 *
ISBN 0 7496 6698 6

TALES OF ROBIN HOOD

Robin and the Knight
ISBN 0 7496 6686 2 *
ISBN 0 7496 6699 4

Robin and the Monk
ISBN 0 7496 6687 0 *
ISBN 0 7496 6700 1

Robin and the Friar
ISBN 0 7496 6688 9 *
ISBN 0 7496 6702 8

Robin and the Silver Arrow
ISBN 0 7496 6689 7 *
ISBN 0 7496 6703 6

*** hardback**